Inept & Random
Thoughts Captured in Haiku

Brett C. Persson

Inept & Random Thoughts Captured in Haiku

X

@BrettCPersson

www.brettcpersson.com

Nudous Publishing, LLC

www.nudouspublishing.com
info@nudouspublishing.com

Paperback ISBN: 978-1-964793-89-4

Dedication

To my loving family and all of those who have supported me along the way.

01/28/2022

I have published other poetry books that I mainly wrote while drinking or on drugs. This is not another one of those books this out the world, life, death, love, hate, God, and many other random and useless things that entered the gray matter between my ears.

Hopefully, you find some enjoyment from them. Some of these will make more sense to some than others.

I asked my daughter Sara to do the illustrations for the book. She is a far more talented artist than I am a poet. I hope you enjoy my book of haikus and the art accompanying it.

Thank you for your time,

Brett C. Persson

1

Out Deep In The Black

Searching For My Missing Soul

Lost In My Childhood

2

Fighting At The Gate

Soldiers Marching Their Orders

Bleeding In The Streets

3

Oceans Of The Deep

Cold And Dark Like Her Dead Heart

The Weights Keep Her Down

4

Thunder Booms Louder

Puffs Of Smoke Rise In The Air

Fire Surrounds The Tree

5

Water Still Like Glass

So Smooth And Stationary

Until It Ripples

6

Chair Against The Wall

Freedom From Across The Wall

John With His Mustache

7

Quick Sudden Impact

Crushed In Twisted Steel And Glass

A Dead Morning Wreck

8

People Working Streets

Money Going In And Out

Play The Daily Game

9

Loud Laughter Erupts

People Carelessly Dancing

With Their Family

10

With A Crown Of Thorns

Only Son Dead On A Cross

A Spear In His Side

11

The Warm Summer Breeze

Blowing The Dust Through The Air

Breath Of The Devil

12

Fearless Is He Now

Slowly He Takes The Last Breath

Enter His Kingdom

13

Feeling Of Power

Harnessed From Within Myself

Reaching Out From Me

14

Shivering While Dark

Pain Surging From My Dead Soul

Waiting For The End

15

Water On A Leaf

Life Giving Into The Green

Absorbing Its Life

16

Endless Skies Of Blue

White Clouds Of Serenity

Rays Of Warming Sun

17

Fear Shaking Within

Nervous, Terrified, And Scared

Will She Talk To Me

18

Noose Around The Neck

Soon To Swing From The Gallows

For Crimes Done To Man

19

Lifting Off The Pad

The Future Of What To Come

Reaching Endless Space

20

Rings Shown For The Years

Ragged Scars On Our Tough Bark

The Pain Of Our Life

21

Lost In Our Own Thoughts

The Songs That Live In Our Minds

Play For Sanity

22

Absorbing Knowledge

Searching And Thirsting For More

Expanding Presence

23

Stubbing Your Small Toe

Cursing The World And God Too

Your Family Laughs

24

The Moon In The Sky

Watching Over Mother Earth

A Fragmented Child

25

Creatures Unknown Live

Deep Within The Dark Ocean

Forever Unseen

26

Death Begins Approach

It Descends Onto Our Lives

Starting From Our Birth

27

Bullets Hit Children

Aimed And Pointed By Children

Such A Waste Of Youth

28

Lost In The Forest

Clueless Drones Of Mankind

Blind By Ignorance

29

Do You Feel His Grace

Entering Your Mortal Soul

Can You See The Truth

30

Changing Points Of View

We Get Bolder And Older

Now See What Is There

31

Chain Reactions Of Life

Actions With Repercussions

Rippling The Water

32

The Tide Maybe High

But You Can Keep Moving On

Making It To Shore

33

Eat Bound To A Chair

Pills As The Better Option

A Head In A Box

34

Oh, So Cold And Dark

Trapped In The Locked Basement

His Next Scared Victim

35

Fire Out Of Control

Ragging Deep From Within Him

He Sees Only Red

36

A Feeling So High

Soaring Way Above The Sky

Feeling Free From All

37

Live The Baller Dream

A Dirty Whore On Each Arm

Money In The Bank

38

Smallest Trace Of Life

On A Single Blade Of Grass

The Endless Wonders

39

Racing Down The Street

A Screaming Bat Out Of Hell

Feel Free With The Speed

40

The Wind At Your Back

The Flight Of The Firefly

Soaring Like A Leaf

41

Focused On The Past

Not Seeing The Future Path

Mind Stuck Out Of Gear

42

All Should Try A Form

Art The Expression Of Life

Even Bad Is Good

43

In A Library

Listening To The Silence

Reading Without Words

44

Viewing True Beauty

Seeing What The Soul Contains

Not What Eyes Behold

45

Laying In A Bed

Body Plagued With Disease

Family Nearby

46

Out In New Eden

Traveling Among The Stars

Out In A New World

47

Understanding Death

Not Fearing It When It Comes

No Way To Escape

48

Not Born Of Woman

A Dramatic Tragedy

The Pain Of The Thane

49

The Fox And The Hound

Like The Coyote And Roadrunner

The Hatfields And McCoys

50

Lost In His Own Mind

Trapped And Unable To Speak

Life On The Spectrum

51

Sadness Of The Heart

Reaching Through The Depths Of Time

Some Things Don't End

52

Back In The Old Days

Was No Need For A Safe Place

Just Living Your Life

53

Waiting After Heist

Stuck In The Passenger Car

Need Help From Above

54

Terms Of Enlistment

Follow The Chain Of Command

Through The Fields Of Fire

55

Through All The Ages

Societies May Rise And Fall

An Empire Is Born

56

Man Searching The Sky

Amongst The Stars, He Does Go

Building Out New Worlds

57

A Man Wept Within

His Dead Child Lay In His Arms

Pain Like No Other

58

He Pierced The Darkness

Finally Gone Where He Dream

Few Had Gone Before

59

Brothers On The Line

Deep In The Trenches Of Death

Bound Always By War

60

Hidden Under Desk

Fearing The Cloud Of Mushrooms

Air Raid Sirens Blair

61

Now I Stare At Death

I Own My Fate No Longer

See All My Regrets

62

It's The Beginning

Of Something New, Right, And Bold

The Future To Come

63

Hurt, Tired, And Bleeding

I Awoke In A Forest

My Thoughts Lost Is Pain

64

From Under A Rock

That Sly Bastard Did Creep Out

Cause Grief And Sorrow

65

The Dim Lights Flicker

There Is A Knock At The Door

Pulse Begins To Race

66

Laying Of Asphalt

Hardening The Worlds Life Flow

Smothering Nature

67

Mentoring The Young

Form A Solid Foundation

Giving Them The Tools

68

Bounding In The Door

The Dog Brings In Her Trophy

Show The Dead Rabbit

69

They Stand In A Line

Facing Each Other With Arms

Civil Is Their War

70

Rookie Shook With Fright

He Made Sure His Pack Was Right

What A Way To Die

71

Born Bearing The Mark

Destined To Destroy The Queen

Was Hunted At Birth

72

Lost In The Winter

Traveling The Winding Road

Looking For Shelter

73

A Gun To His Head

Shot Rings Out Shattered Silence

Thinks His Final Thought

74

Woman On Death Row

Jessica Waits For Her Fate

Murderer Convict

75

Jon Lives On The Streets

Avoiding Pressure Of Life

He Chooses His Path

76

Caught In The Moment

Should A Flee Or Should I Fight

The Outcome Unknown

77

Looking For Some Tracks

Walking Down The Riverbank

Searching For A Kill

78

Michael Seems At Peace

Hearing The Voice Of His God

Twisted In His Faith

79

I Hear The Chime Ring

I Feel The Breeze Flow Around

I Feel At Peace

80

Walking On The Beach

Footprints He Follows So Blind

Trusting In His Faith

81

Hanging Vines From Tree

Under The Canopy Woods

The Light Barely Shows

82

Once Had Now Is Gone

Stability Of The Mind

Age Caught Up To Time

83

Sitting On The Bus

The Damn Chicken Clucks And Squawks

He Had Blocked It Out

84

Awoke From A Dream

A Life Is Lived While Asleep

My First Wife Still Here

85

He Hears A Gun Shot

People Run Around The Street

A Child Dies This Night

86

Dressed As An Old Drag

Burning Fire He Has No Doubt

Hairy Legs On Bus

87

Emergency One

Always Ready And Waiting

Rushing To The Scene

88

Turn The Beat Around

Listen To That Awful Sound

In Your Head, It's Bound

89

Shoot Up In The Vein

Nodding Out During The Drive

A Little Too Much

90

Finding A Target

One Incoming Missile

Hideout Destroyed

91

A Wide Gravel Path

Leading From The Village Square

The Prancing Pony

92

Counter-Rotating

First Helicopter On Mars

Ingenuity

93

Ran Out On A Rail

Dumped By The Roadside Alive

No Tar, No Feathers

94

The Camera Clicks

Shutter Flies Open And Closed

Image Now Preserved

95

Tip The Bottle Back

Willpower I Use To Lack

Sober Now For Ten

96

Out In The Jungle

Orange Is A Death Agent

Men Were Sacrificed

97

Hermes Rotates

Heading Home And Back Again

Such A Long Journey

98

Hear The Record Play

Play That Old Vinyl Again

That Crackle And Hiss

99

Once I Did A Fast

Twenty-Seven Days Did Last

On Water And Hope

100

Not Fearing His Death

Just The Process Of Dying

Hope For Peaceful Rest

101

Stained Glass Church Windows

White Doves Flying Threw Clouds

Gods Light Shining Down

102

Tattoos Depict Art

Of Freedom And Thought Expressed

Canvas Of The Skin

103

It's A No-hitter

It's For The Love Of The Game

Playing The Last Game

104

Johnny Grab Your Gun

Start Shooting Them As They Run

Bully Now In Sights

105

Stranded On A Boat

Skirting The Florida Coast

Seeking Asylum

106

Sputnik Satellite

Two Nations Fight For Power

The Final Frontier

107

Sally Ride Space Vet

Setting The Bar For Women

First Women In Space

108

Fighting For Freedom

An American Hero

Saving Others Lives

109

Fighting In A War

Hunting In The Dense Jungle

Enemy Unknown

110

Suicide Painless

Changes It Does Bring

Take It Or Leave It

111

Stressed After Flying

Crinkling His Toes In Carpet

On The Thirty Floor

112

Living In A Dream

My Life Is My Delusion

I Live It My Way

113

The Voices He Hears

Always Talking In His Ear

Guide Him In His Thoughts

114

Hands Covered In Blood

A Dark Grisly Homicide

Joyous Feeling Right

115

A Childhood Shattered

Lost In Pain And Grief Of Death

Loss Of Her Parents

116

Watching The Fan Spin

Feeling Its Cool Gentle Breeze

Relaxing In Shade

117

Light Shinning On Soul

His Grace Entering The Heart

Salvation He Gets

118

The Gentle Giant

He Scares Them With His Size

Judged By Appearance

119

Caught In The Middle

Fighting For The Right Of Child

All Side Losing Sight

120

Fingers Down Her Throat

Feeling Ugly And Ashamed

Purging Food And Soul

121

Rain Of The Gray Mist

The Darkness Of Something Wet

Lost From Sight And Sound

122

Riding The Black Bull

Bucking And Fighting The Ride

Eight Seconds To Win

123

Phone Begins To Ring

Called In The Middle Of Night

Their Only Child Dead

124

Covering The Spread

Shaving The Points, He Needed

Collecting The Check

125

Minding My Own Self

A Disaster Strikes Again

Me Without A Knife

126

Life In The Fast Lane

Speeding By Moments In Time

Regretting Things Lost

127

Extended Mission

Five Hundred Thirty-Three Days

All To Rescue Him

128

The Giver Of Life

His Grace Bestowed Upon Man

Sacrificed His Son

129

Got To Get My Jam

Leaning On My Radio

Let Music Move You

130

The Sight Of A Tree

Plants Bloom Full Of All Colors

Sounds Of Animals

131

Red Dust On The Ground

A Possible Future Home

Devoid Of All Life

132

Married With Children

Most From Having Family

Living A Full Life

133

Money Moving Fast

Spending It Like I Got It

My Cycle Of Debt

134

Destined To Be More

Kept Fighting Myself For Years

Potential Is Lost

135

Shadow Break Of Day

An Eternal Fear Life Is

Enjoying The Death

136

Forties And Fifties

Harry Truman President

Doris Day Actress

137

Ruined Other Lives

A Communist Subversion

Joseph McCarthy

138

President Nixon

Vietnam Peace With Honor

Watergate Scandal

139

The Atom Spy Case

Targeted The Rosenbergs

Their Execution

140

G Santayana

A Poet Of Rhythm And Rhyme

A Philosopher

141

Egyptian Nasser

An Almost Near Bloodless Coup

Second President

142

Roy Campanella

Negro And Mexican Legue

A Baseball Legend

143

Cool James Byron Dean

Car Cartwheeling Like A Child

Dead From Racers Road

144

Be A Simple Man

My Father Told Me Once

Troubles Come And Pass

145

Your Eyes Don't See Me
I Can't Play With You No More
On The Darker Side

146

The L.A. Blue Jeans
Pretty Smile Dancing In Sand
No One Near To Hear

147

God Is Wrong Sometimes

Gives More Than You Can Handle

Suicide Way Out

148

Name What Would You See

Viewing On Moment Of Time

Jesus On A Cross

149

Told I Was Stupid

Struggled With Learning Basics

Wasted Potential

150

Unpredictable

Another Fork Stuck Ahead

Choosing A New Path

151

Feeling All Life's Pain

Screaming Out In The Darkness

Tearing At Your Soul

152

Boots Filled With Their Blood

Fighting Their Way Into Hell

Troopers Of The Dead

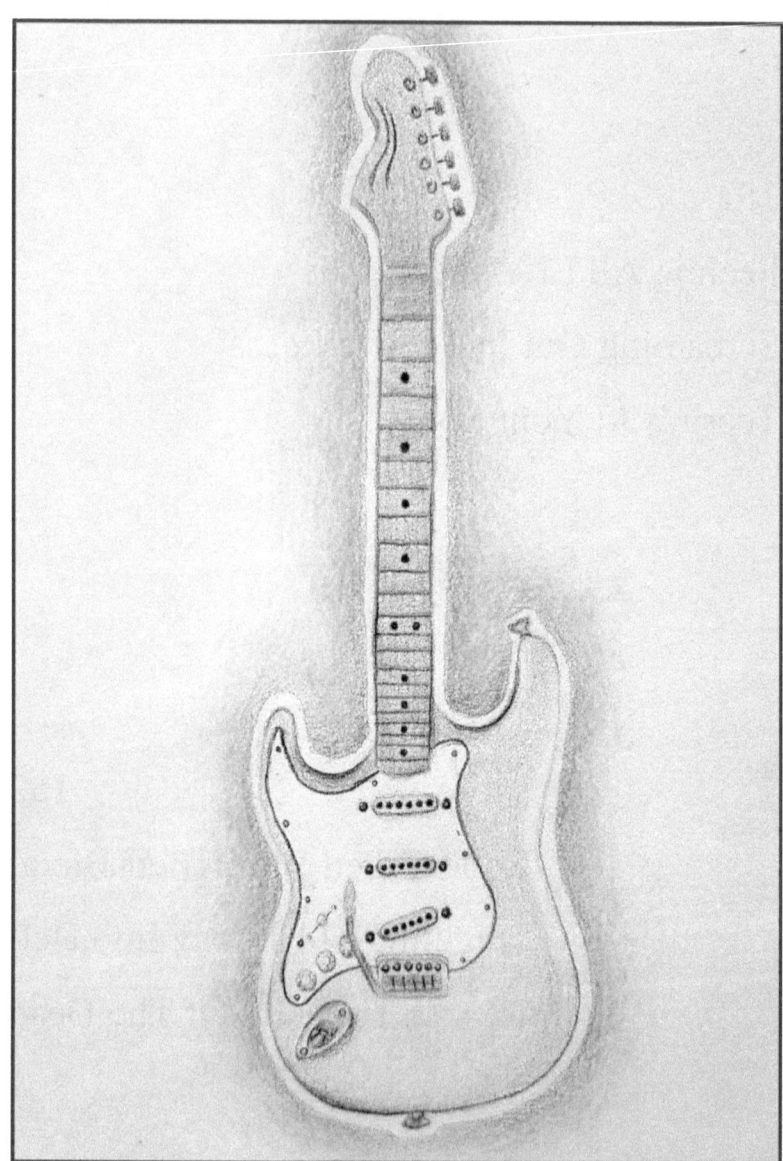

153

Left-Handed Guitar

Died On The Day Of My Birth

Rest In Peace Jimi

154

My Infinite Dreams

Flooding My Minds Eye At Night

Satan At The Door

155

I Take The Last Breath

Darkness Clouding My Vision

The Eternal Sleep

156

Wonder If I'm Free

Trying To Hold My Head Up

Too Blind To See True

157

Life Is A Razor

Balancing On The Life's Edge

A Blade On The Wrist

158

Freedom Of The Heart

Peace Of The Soul And The Mind

Love Everlasting

159

Stars Charlton Heston

Merchant In Jerusalem

Jewish Prince Ben Hur

160

Edsel A No-Go

Named After Henry Ford's Son

Wrong Car At Wrong Time

161

The U-2 Spy Plane

Shot By Soviet Missile

Powers Prisoner

162

Chubby Checkers Twist

Hitchcock's Psycho Bates Thriller

Syngman Rhee Resigns

163

Dylan Folk Music

Ernest Commits Suicide

Soviets Build Wall

164

Stuck On Firey Plane

Plummeting Towards The Ground

Praying For Safety

165

Singing Of Angels

Grace Of God Captured In Song

Voice Of Salvation

166

Best That I Can Be

Going To Find Solution

Prove It To Myself

167

Dew On A Leaf Dries

Wind Carries The Smell Of Death

The Singing Bird Dies

168

Student Meredith

First Admitted To Ole Miss

Integrate The School

169

British Sex Scandal

Secretary Profumo

Affair With Keeler

170

Aids, The Gay Cancer

Early Reports Say This Much

Plague Set On Depraved

171

Living Life Sober

Progress Over Perfection

One Day At A Time

172

We Shall Not Perish

Gave The World His Only Son

Whoever Believes

173

Lord Is My Shepherd

I Lie Down In Green Pastures

He Restores My Soul

174

No God Before Me

Nothing Found In Afterlife

No Faith, No Belief

175

No Special Talent

Passionately Curious

Albert Einstein Says

176

Demons Are At Bay

I Don't Know What Is To Come

No Dope, Just Some Hope

177

Running With A Gun

To Get Away From The Scene

Live Another Day

178

His Future Is Bleak

A Gun Pressed Under His Chin

He Sees No Way Out

179

Drinking At A Bar

Cannot Walk And Cannot Talk

Faculties So Gone

180

It Was Big And Blue

Written By A Friend Named Bill

It Saved Countless Souls

181

Shots Killing The Tots

Hear The War Killing The Poor

Death In City Streets

182

People Living Life

No Winners, Just Us Sinners

Riding It To Hell

183

Who Is This Stranger

Invoking Relentless Hate

Fuck, It's A Mirror

184

The Air Tastes So Sweet

The Gentle Breeze Blowing West

The Smell Of The Grass

185

You Don't Have To Hide

Behind A Mask Or Yourself

Just Show Who You Are

186

Beaten With A Stick

Dragged Behind A Speeding Car

Swinging From A Tree

187

The Snow Is Falling

Blowing In Heavy And Deep

Nose Begins To Bleed

188

The Past Is Alive

I Am Losing Who I Am

Reality Lost

189

Visions Of My Life

Memories Of The Past Night

Distorted Lost Dreams

190

Autopilot On

Struggles Of The Modern Man

No Ambition Left

191

Letting Your Soul Soar

Being Open To His Grace

Feel His Awesome Grace

192

You Will Be Just Fine

People Don't Need A Safe Place

They Need To Be Strong

193

Listen To The Voice

Your Life Shatters Like A Dish

Your Last Dying Breath

194

In From The Ocean

See The Storm Coming In Fast

Shelter From Danger

195

Laying In A Bed

My Heart Rate Slow, My Breath Low

Slipping Into Death

196

On Stool Drinking Beer

Where Everyone Knows Your Name

It Is Where I Go

197

Number Of The Beast

Eddie Always There Rising

Stranger In Strange Land

198

Black Abyss Waiting

Traveling Around Abound

Shooting For The Stars

199

Feeling The Sands Drift

Time Slipping Between Fingers

Forever To Dust

200

Unidentified

Oversensitivity

Personality

201

I Yawn In The Dawn

Rub My Eyes As I Arise

I Crack My Old Back

202

Station Five Miles Long

It's The Last Best Hope For Peace

A Dream Given Form

203

Speeding Through My Life

Dodging The Strife Best, I Can

Better Fast Than Good

204

The Bark Of A Tree

The Skin Of Woman And Man

The Hide Of The Wild

205

Best Care Anywhere

The Four O Double Seven

Surgical Legends

206

Locked In A Soft Room

People In Lab Coats Watch Me

Sanity Challenged

207

Flashing Blue And Red

Sirens Fill The Dark Night Air

Sounds Of The City

208

Green Grass Underfoot

The Wind Whistles Around Me

Canopy Of Trees

209

Reaching For Something

Not Able To Make A Grasp

Always Out Of Reach

210

His Life Lost To Drugs

His Breathing Stopped During Sleep

His Addiction Won

211

Pastor Of The Lost

Trying To Save The Lost Souls

A Soldier Of Christ

212

Figuring Out Life

Being Okay With Oneself

Is True Happiness

213

The Friends Of Your Youth

Can Drift Away Through The Years

Time Can Be Ruthless

214

Out In The Nature

Seeing The Beauty Of Life

Feeling Mother Earth

215

Small Cup Of Chili

He Is Uncomfortable

Unspoken Meeting

216

A Ship Deep In Space

The Soul Of The Icarus

Searching Out The Stars

217

Little Green Beings

Rocketing And Exploding

Getting To The Mun

218

Today's Dying Youth

Troubled, Lost, And Addicted

The Drugs Plague Holds Them

219

The Needle Slides In

Feel The Buzz Of The Machine

Tattooed Life Begins

220

Prisoners Asleep

Walking The Dark Corridors

The Guard's Watchful Eye

221

The Storm Coming In

The Waves Crash Onto The Shore

Hurricane Looms Large

222

Tell No One At All

Some Secrets Must Be Held Close

Take It To Your Grave

223

Reckless Emotions

Scattered Thoughts And Scattered Mind

High, Highs And Low, Lows

224

The Detective Stares

Clicks His Pen And Does Not Blink

Waiting For The Lies

225

Me Being Selfish

Taking Care Of Myself First

Sober Lives Matter

226

Station Five Miles Long

It's The Last Best Hope For Peace

A Dream Given Form

227

Rolling With My Girl

Many Hours Of The Night Spent

Talking Long And Deep

228

A Cross Made Of Wood

Crucified And Sacrificed

Died For The Sinners

229

Feeling What I Feel

Being Okay With Myself

Living My Best Life

230

A Woman Named White

Laughing Her Way Into Hearts

Rest In Peace Betty

231

Lost Too Young In Life

My Sobriety, His Birth

Always Remember

232

Dreams I Once Held High

Things I Wanted To Become

The Things That I Am

233

The Sea Holds His Soul

Captain Of His Destiny

A Sailor From Birth

234

Lost In Random Thought

Mind Wonders And Leaps Around

Don't Listen To You

235

The Earth Was Used Up

Central Alliance Planets

Rise Of The Browncoats

236

Vala Mal Doran

The Peacekeeper Aeryn Sun

Audrey MaCallum

237

Ever Brought You Joy

Or Only Heartache And Loss

Love A Troubled Thing

238

Yeah, I Got One Too

An Opinion Of The Mind

Does Not Mean I'm Right

239

Rocks Covered In Moss

The Leaves Wet With Morning Dew

Grass Moving In Wind

240

A Feeling I Get

Through The Tree A Songbird Sings

I Look To The West

241

Electric Dance Moves

Lightning-Fast Flashing Strobe Lights

Psychedelic Groove

242

Volleyball Player

Blonde Hair Over Bold Blue Eyes

Scandinavian

243

Noah, Born A Crime

South African Apartheid

Rises To Success

244

Standing On A Ledge

Seeing The Traffic Below

Long Fall Down, Quick Stop

245

The Church Bells Ring Out

In Fellowship Together

Making Their Way In

246

Making My Way Home

Try Doing The Next Right Thing

The Straight And Narrow

247

Falling Into It

Scrambling To Find A Way Out

Finding A Meaning

248

See The Sun Up High

Engulfed By Its Shinning Light

Feel Its Warmth Inside

249

Twelve Thousand Feet Up

Soaring Like A Bird In Flight

The Ground Rushing Up

250

The Fairy Dances

Around Fire On A Cold Night

Laughing Into Night

251

Looking For A Piece

Marion Says Abner Died

A Fire Burns Bar Down

252

The Ocean Bottom

Holds The Lost Titanic Souls

Trapped Forever So

253

Covered In White Snow

Standing On A Mountain Top

I Can See The World

254

Learn To Calm Thyself

Spiritual Peace Of Mind

Enveloping You

255

Bricks Make The Road Long

It Twists And Turns Without Cause

No Exit From It

256

Single Blade Of Grass

Countless Forms Of Life Around

A Forest Of Trees

257

Allow What Life Is

Strive To Understand And Learn

Give Back More Than Take

258

First To Land, Red Moon

Shackleton Crater Landing

Pathfinder Showdown

259

A Lump In Her Breast4

Disbelief And Shock Soon Start

Panic Takes Its Hold

260

Political Woes

Challenge Each Other As Foes

Both Are Full Of Shit

261

Swayze, Mercury

Ramis, Ritter, Diana

Gandhi, Theresa

262

Just Forget Regret

You Cannot Change What Is Done

Keep Moving Forward

263

Back From Bloody War

Forever Changed To The Core

The Price Of Freedom

264

Radio Static

Waiting For Conformation

Silently Waiting

265

I Do Dream In Sleep

They Are Grand By My Design

My Own World Be True

266

I Cry For Her Loss

I Weep For Their Hurt Loved Ones

Death Can Come Early

267

Life Events Change You

Shape The Person You Will Be

For Better Or Worse

268

Nineteen Eighty-Six

Challenger Disaster Strikes

Touch The Face Of God

269

Legend Bill Shatner

James Kirk, TekWar, Space Command

A Sci-Fi Hero

270

Garrett Ride Them Down

The Young Gun Is On The Run

Friendship Turned Bounty

271

A White Wedding Dress

Friends And Family Gather

New Life Together

272

Momma Used To Say

From Under What Rock Was He

Remember, I Can't

273

Reaching For Something

Trying To Find What I Lack

Still Not Knowing What

274

The Gavel Hits Hard

Guilty For His Heinous Crime

The Sentenced Passed Down

275

World Of Confusion

People Move As Mindless Drones

The Pace Of New Life

276

Out In The Blackness

Fleeing The Alliance Grasp

We Ain't Looking Back

277

Will Always Be Free

Cannot Take The Sky From Us

Not With Serenity

278

That Makes Us Mighty

Not A Fancy Gentleman

But Big Damn Heros

279

On The Losing Side

Valley They Did Surrender

We Still Were Not Wrong

280

Living My Good Life

A Middle-Class Family

Parents Did Me Right

281

Cleared My Darkest Days

Found The End Of My Darkness

Returned To A Life

282

Absolute Horror

Where My Life Could Have Gone To

Seen As I Look Back

283

Touched By The Chosen

Made The King Of The New Realm

Lorkian Rises

284

Locked In A Battle

Fighting For My Survival

The Swords Clash And Clang

285

Dogs Bark The Wolves Howl

Calling Out Into The Night

Beasts Still All The Same

286

Ledger, Marley, Dean

Joplin, Hendrix, Morrison

Cobain, Keats, Phoenix

287

Proud Of Who I Am

Come Down A Long Winding Road

Found My Way Years Late

288

Life In The Balance

Going To Be Touch And Go

People Always Pray

289

Elizabeth Died

A Troubled Start To His Life

Married First Cousin

290

First Published At Nine

Suicide Attempt First Failed

She Died Where Yeats Lived

291

Harlem Renaissance

A Poet Of The People

He Worked With Woodson

292

All The Lights Go Out

The World Goes Into Darkness

An Apocalypse

293

Rain Begins To Fall

Snow Begins On A Cold Day

Melts In The Summer

294

He Married Bree Stone

Janelle, Damon And Ali

Faithful In The 'Cross'

295

Approaching The End

Wondering What Lies Beyond

Finding Out What's Next

296

I Stretch My Back Out

Muscles Are Sore, My Bones Ache

A Good Day To Live

297

Time Catches Us All

Never Stops Ticking By Us

 Death Always Closer

298

They Buried The Dead

Graves With A Simple Marker

Returned To Their God

299

Seeing Open Gates

Knowing Salvation Is Here

A True Believer

300

Is This The Ending

I Believe Our Time Is Done

I Hope You Liked It

ABOUT THE AUTHOR

Born in 1973, Brett C Persson is an aspiring poet and recovering alcoholic who crafts his experiences into thought-provoking poetry and prose. As the author of his debut book, "Poetry Of An Addict" and several other collections, Brett hopes to provide readers with poignant insights into the life of an ex-addict as he ranges across universal themes through descriptive wordplay and vivid imagery. He aims to reassure readers struggling with alcoholism that they're not alone, helping them find solace in poetry's unique and expressive power. Brett resides in Buckeye, Arizona, with his wonderful wife and three daughters.

11/14/11